First published in Great Britain 2020 by Walker Books Ltd
87 Vauxhall Walk, London SE11 5HJ

This edition published 2022

Published by arrangement with Tundra Books, a division of Penguin Random House Canada Limited

2 4 6 8 10 9 7 5 3 1

© 2020 Anne Hunter

This text was hand lettered by Anne Hunter

Printed in China

British Library Cataloguing in Publication Data:
a catalogue record for this book is available from the British Library

ISBN 978-1-4063-9425-2

www.walker.co.uk

This Walker book belongs to:

....

....

....

Anne Hunter

Where's Baby?

WALKER BOOKS
AND SUBSIDIARIES
LONDON • BOSTON • SYDNEY • AUCKLAND

Hi, Papa!
Can we do that again?

Anne Hunter is a Geisel Honor–awarded illustrator
and picture book writer best known for her books about animals
and nature. Anne grew up in Lake Worth, Florida, and now
makes her home with the foxes and the owls and the skunks
and her family in the woods of Southern Vermont, USA.
Find her online at annehunterstudio.com and on Instagram
at @annehunterillustration.

Available at all good booksellers

www.walker.co.uk